I am Josephine

(and I am a living thing)

To my parents, for first teaching me that I am an animal and then telling me not to act like one. — J.T.

Many thanks to all my friends, new and old. — J.L.

Franklin Watts

First published in Great Britain in 2017 by
The Watts Publishing Group

Text © 2016 Jan Thornhill
Illustrations © 2016 Jacqui Lee

Published by permission of Owlkids Books Inc., Toronto, Ontario, Canada.

The artwork in this book was created in watercolor and assembled digitally.
Edited by: Karen Li
Designed by: Karen Powers

ISBN 978 1 4451 5224 0

Manufactured in Dongguan, China, in May 2016, by Toppan Leefung Packaging & Printing (Dongguan) Co., Ltd.
Job #BAYDC23

Franklin Watts
An imprint of Hachette Children's Group
Part of the Watts Publishing Group
Carmelite House
50 Victoria Embankment
London EC4Y 0DZ

An Hachette UK Company
www.hachette.co.uk

www.franklinwatts.co.uk

I am Josephine

(and I am a living thing)

Written by
Jan Thornhill

Illustrations by
Jacqui Lee

W

FRANKLIN WATTS
LONDON • SYDNEY

I am Josephine.

I am Josephine, and
I am a human being.

I am a **human being**, and so is my mum,
and so is my dad, and so is my baby brother, Felix.

BUS
STOP

CITY BUS

How many **human beings** can you find on this page?

I am Josephine,
and I am a mammal.

I am a **mammal**, and so is my mum,
and so is my dog, Cosmo, and so is a squirrel.

And so is that cat that's always
following me around. (Shoo, kitty!)

How many different kinds of **mammals** can you find on this page?

I am Josephine,
and I am an animal.

I am an **animal**, and so is my dad,
and so is a fish, and so is a deer, and so is
that mosquito that just bit me. (Ouch!)

How many different kinds of **animals**
can you find on this page?

I am Josephine,
and I am a living thing.

I am a **living thing**, and so is my brother, Felix, and so is a butterfly, and so is a tree, and so is a penguin.

How many different kinds of **living things** can you find on this page?

I am Josephine.

I am a human being.

I am a mammal.

I am an animal.

I am a living thing.

I am **all** of these things.

But I am still the only **me**—
Josephine!

Living things

* are made up of one or more tiny cells

* grow

* make copies of themselves (have babies)

* react to things around them

* need water and food (some make food from the Sun's energy)

* get rid of waste

* move in some way

Animals are living things that

* usually have a mother and a father (though many never know who their mothers and fathers are)

* eat other living things

* digest food in a "stomach"

* can usually move around freely

Mammals are animals that

* usually have four legs
  (or two arms and two legs
  or flippers)

* give birth to live young (except
  for a few that lay eggs)

* feed their babies milk

* have hair or fur

* have warm blood

Human beings are mammals that

* stand upright

* walk on two legs

* can do many things with their
  hands and fingers

* have large busy brains

* talk to one another about
  a million different things

* remember what happened yesterday
  and imagine what might happen
  tomorrow

* make and use complicated tools

* make art and music for the
  pure joy of it

Josephine is a human being...and so are you.

Every human being is unique, which means there is no one else on Earth who is exactly like you!

What makes you different from other human beings?